Tales of the
Texas Mermaid
"The Boot"

Written and Illustrated by Mary Borgia
Goretti Publishing
✦ San Antonio, Texas ✦

2-14-07 Jms,
Happy Reading to You!
Blessings,
Mary Borgia

a TEXAS MERMAID production

Tales of the Texas Mermaid
"The Boot"
Copyright © 2006 by Mary Borgia
Printed in China

Library of Congress Control Number: 2006922086

International Standard Book Number: 0-9778451-0-9-Hardcover

Goretti Publishing

First Edition

10 9 8 7 6 5 4 3 2 1

In loving memory of my great grandfathers and their fellow drovers of Texas longhorn cattle.

"Tell us more! Where was she from? What was she like?" Girls and boys of all ages could hardly wait to learn more about the Texas Mermaid. Blarney, the Texas longhorn, knew the whole story.

A few weeks earlier, Blarney told his friend Woodring the mermaid's story. Woodring thought children should hear these tales before they were lost forever.

A little mouse named Albert overheard the longhorns' conversation. Texas mice cannot keep a secret and so Albert whispered news of the story to every girl and boy in Texas.

One day as Blarney strolled through town for his daily exercise, a group of children ran behind him, begging to hear about this little girl from the past. Blarney hadn't planned on telling his story, but with the children clamoring to find out more, he had no choice.

"Yes, yes. Y'all gather around and I'll tell you about the dear little lass." The children gathered around Blarney in a nearby stable and watched the old longhorn yank a blade of grass from the crusted earth. He cleared his throat, placed the blade of grass between his teeth, kicked back against a comfortable rock, and began his tale.

"The story begins with a spunky young cowgirl named Cecilia. My granddad Scottie met her in San Antonio, Texas. She was the friendliest person you would ever meet and she never went anywhere without her parrot Amigo."

Blarney shifted his hips and crossed his legs, "Now Cecilia's grandfather led a cattle drive from Texas up the Western Trail. Each spring, Cecilia went along as they trailed cattle northward. The job proved risky and the work hard, but Cecilia looked forward to the adventure."

"Wait a minute," one of the children said. "I mean, excuse me Blarney, but what was so risky about a cattle drive?"

Blarney replied, "Well, cowboys had to drive the longhorn cattle through rivers, storms, and dangerous territory. A strange noise might startle the cattle and they'd stampede. When thunderstorms rolled over the open range, bolts of lightening lit up the sky and thunder shook the ground. If a cowboy wasn't careful, a bolt of lightning might just light up the very breeches he was wearing! And when I get on with my story you'll learn about some of the outlaws a cowboy could expect to meet on the trail."

Billy jumped to his knees and raised his hand, "Why would Cecilia look forward to all that?"

Blarney chuckled. "There was plenty for Cecilia to look forward to. She loved riding her horse across the country and meeting new people. At the end of the day she couldn't wait to meet up with the chuck wagon for dinner. The smell of bacon and beans made her stomach rumble. Cecilia and the cowboys would eat their grub around the campfire, tell stories, and sing cowboy songs."

"But most of all Cecilia liked spending time with her granddad. Granddad Brown taught Cecilia how to fish and skip rocks across the river. Why, that tough old cowboy even taught her how to pray."

"Now I want to tell you about the cattle drive that changed Cecilia's life forever." Blarney adjusted his glasses and looked at each child. "After breakfast one morning, Granddad Brown shouted to everyone, 'Saddle Up!'"

"A dozen riders mounted their horses and were ready to go when a pair of Texas Rangers rode into camp. One of them said, 'Mr. Brown, I need to talk to you!'

Granddad wheeled his horse around. 'Whoa there, girl!' He recognized an old friend who wore the star of the Texas Rangers. 'How can I help you Captain Barnes?'

Captain Barnes and his sergeant reined in their horses and the captain shook Granddad's hand. 'We're on the hunt for a mean band of cattle rustlers and we've tracked them to this part of Texas.'

The Rangers showed Granddad posters of the wanted men and the captain said, 'We've been chasing these thieves for two weeks with no luck. We'd like to follow behind y'all for a day or so in case the rustlers decide to stir up some trouble.'"

"Now these rustlers ran into their own trouble on their way to Texas. They had stopped in a Kansas ghost town for a rest when they stumbled upon a pile of brand new cowboy boots. The leader of the group, named Lucky, said, 'I say we take these boots for ourselves and hightail it out of here!' Lucky and his gang loaded the boots into their saddlebags and headed for Texas."

"A few days later, the rustlers set up camp on the banks of a river. After unloading the gear, they could hardly wait to try on their new boots. Lucky complained, 'These boots are too tight. That extra pair looks like they might fit.' But when he tried to pull off the new boots, they were stuck. The outlaws each tugged on Lucky's boots, but the boots would not budge. Then they tried to remove their own boots, but their boots were stuck too! 'Dad gummite!' Lucky shouted, 'These boots must be cursed!' He threw the leftover pair of boots behind a boulder along the edge of the river.

Homer, one of the gang, jumped to his feet. 'Ah, come on Lucky. Never mind about the boots. We've gotta make ready to steal some of them cattle that are comin' our way.' Lucky agreed and the greedy men devised a plan to ambush Granddad Brown and his herd."

"Meanwhile, the Texas Rangers rode to the rear of the herd and Granddad Brown hollered to get the cowboys and longhorns moving. They rode all day until they came to a wide river where the cattle could drink and rest. When Cecilia reached the river bank, a snake slithered through the high grass and spooked Buster, her horse. Buster bucked wildly and sent her tumbling behind the rock where Lucky had thrown that last pair of mysterious boots."

"She landed with both legs smack inside a large sized boot. 'Oh no! I can't get my legs out! I'm stuck!' With Amigo and Buster watching, she struggled to free herself from the boot, but it wouldn't come loose."

"Just when things seemed hopeless, a low gruff voice asked, 'Well, well what do we have here?' Cecilia looked up and recognized the men she'd seen on the wanted posters.

Cecilia replied, 'No, what do I have here?' She pulled her lariat from Buster's saddle, lassoed the bad guys, and kept 'em tied up while Amigo flew for help.

The longhorns passed Amigo's urgent cries to Granddad Brown, who understood longhorn talk. Granddad galloped to Cecilia's side and Amigo flew off to find the Texas Rangers, who came and dragged them rustlers off to jail."

"When the Texas Rangers learned the story behind the mysterious boots, Captain Barnes had to break some grim news to Cecilia. 'Darlin', that there boot will never come off your legs. I'm afraid you'll be stuck in it the rest of your life.'

'I don't understand Captain Barnes,' Cecilia stared at him, puzzled.

'A traveling cobbler named Claude made that there boot. He knew how much cowboys loved their boots and wanted to make the perfect fit cowboy boot. His experiment failed. Instead, he made a bunch of boots that would never come off once they touched the feet of a real cowboy or cowgirl. He ditched those boots in a ghost town thinking no one would ever find them. Unfortunately, Lucky and his gang took the boots for their own and you had the misfortune to fall into one of them.'"

"Cecilia thought for a moment, and then replied, 'Well, I guess I'll have to make the best of it then.'

That's when she enlisted the help of my Granddad Scottie. Cecilia learned to ride sidesaddle, and with a little help from Scottie and Amigo, she did everything just as well as before her little mishap."

"Blarney! Blarney! What ever happened to the other large boot?   Was it left behind the boulder near the river?" asked Susie.

"Don't you little ones worry. The Rangers destroyed the last boot and the cobbler promised to never make another boot of that kind."

"From that day on, Cecilia was known as The Texas Mermaid. Though her life changed forever, she could hardly wait for her next adventure."

Blarney stopped talking and sniffed the air. The delicious smell of grass filled his nostrils. He looked at the sun, because that's how longhorns judge the time of the day, and grumbled, "It's five o'clock, children. I'm fixin' to eat my supper right now. You'll have to come back later to hear another tale."

Blarney flicked his tail, stretched his long legs, and ambled down the dusty road to meet Woodring for supper.

Now longhorns tend to procrastinate, especially in the hot Texas weather; but don't you worry children, Albert, the Texas mouse, will make sure that old longhorn tells another tale of the Texas Mermaid.